Another Sneeze, Louise!

written by
Cheryl A. Potts

illustrated by
Gloria Gedeon

KAEDEN ❤ BOOKS™

Louise likes to play outside.

"Achoo!"

sneezed Louise.

She likes to pick wild
flowers.

She likes to climb trees.

7

She likes to pet the kitten.

"Achoo!"

"Another sneeze, Louise!"

9

She likes to blow the dandelions.

11

She likes to roll in the grass.

13

"Aaaaaachoo!"

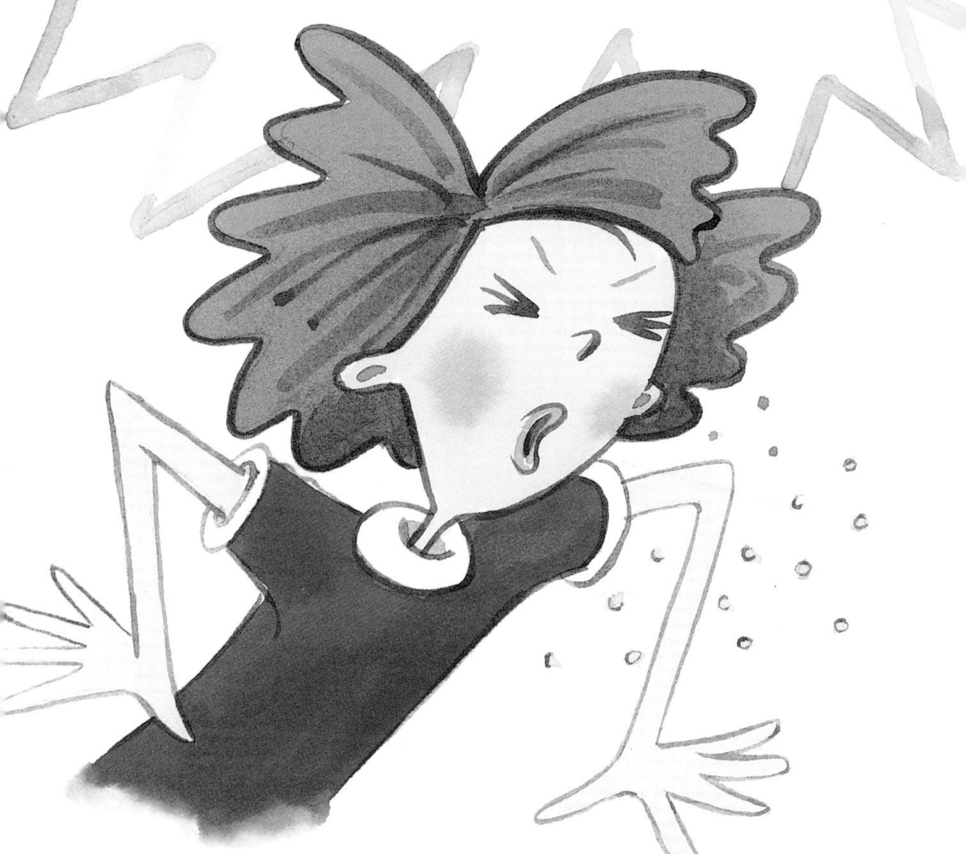

"Oh please! Help Louise with her allergies."